LET'S GO TO THE ARCTIC

A Story and Activities About Arctic People and Animals

By Charlotte Ford Mateer

with Louise Craft

Illustrated by Linda Witt Fries

The Carnegie Museum of Natural History
and Roberts Rinehart Publishers

This publication was made possible throught the support of the Benedum Endowment for Education and the Scaife Family Foundation.

The author wishes to acknowledge the following people: Louise Craft, friend and editor at The Carnegie Museum of Natural History, whose experience, enthusiasm, and patience brought this book to completion; Kristin Kovacic, for her guidance and expertise, so generously given, in the art of writing; Susan Rowley, whose first-hand knowledge of the Arctic and its people brought an important perspective to this undertaking and vital technical accuracy; Judith Bobenage, chairman of the museum's Division of Education, for her support of this project; Helene Tremaine, of The Carnegie Library of Pittsburgh, for suggestions and guidelines on books for young readers; and, finally, Donald Mateer, for his constant support and encouragement.

Design by Louise Craft

The poem on page 16, "Walrus-Hunting" by Aua, is from *Poems of the Inuit,* edited by John Robert Colombo, by permission of Oberon Press.

Published in the United States of America by Roberts Rinehart Publishers
Post Office Box 666, Niwot, Colorado 80544-0666

Published in Great Britain, Ireland, and Europe by Roberts Rinehart Publishers
3 Bayview Terrace, Schull, West Cork, Republic of Ireland

Published in Canada by Key Porter Books
70 The Esplanade, Toronto, Ontario M5E 1R2

International Standard Book Number 1-879373-24-6

Manufactured in the United States of America

Contents

Setting the Scene

You are about to travel to the past! It will be a fast trip so hold on and shut your eyes as you fly back in time to the year 1900. After you screech to a stop, prepare to visit the Canadian Arctic. The dogs are hitched to the sledge waiting to carry you over icy sea and snowy land, so bundle up in your fur parka, boots, and trousers. How do you look? Flip to the front cover to find out.

You don't need to crack your whip over the dogs' heads. They know they are almost home and need no reminder to run fast. Look, a snowhouse . . . and some children are waving. It's your friend Qajaq and his sister Ukpijuak! The dogs' feet hardly touch the crisp, white snow as they race. Even the puppy, running hard beside the team as he trains to join them, is eager to reach home . . . and his dinner.

Get ready to spend time with an Inuit family. Inuit (IN-u-eat), means "the people" and is what these people call themselves. You may know them as Eskimo--that's what they used to be called. You'll discover how the Inuit lived and learn more about the Arctic, too.

Here's how to pronounce the names of the people in the story:

Son: Qajaq (KAI-yak)
   (His name means "kayak.")
Daughter: Ukpijuak (OOK-pik-jew-ack)
   (Her name means "Snowy Owl.")
Mother: Natsiq (NAT-serk)
Father: Maniq (MAN-erk)
Baby Sister: Aua (AH-wah)
Puppy: Piujuq (Pee-OO-yuck)
Cousin: Amarualik (ah-MAH-roo-ah-lick)
Qajaq's Friend: Ivalu (ee-VAH-loo)
Ukpijuak's Friend: Ilupalik (ee-loo-PAH-lick)
Uncle: Qatalik (KAH-tah-lick)

Tell Me, Wind

October on Baffin Island

Qajaq wanted to escape. For three days the Inuit family had been held prisoner inside their tent by the fierce wind and swirling snow. Qajaq held the flap of the skin shelter open and struggled to see the distant hills that rose above the flat, treeless tundra. The kaleidoscope of white flakes kept clouding his view. No hills, no caribou passing in search of food. Even the dogs sleeping nearby were hidden, curled beneath soft blankets of snow.

"Ugh!" he said in disgust, letting the flap close with such a *thrap* that Natsiq, his mother, lifted her head from her sewing.

Maniq, Qajaq's father, continued carving as he sat silently on the skin-covered earth floor.

Grandfather stopped singing and eyed his impatient ten-year-old grandson. Then he closed his eyes and continued his soft song.

Ukpijuak, Qajaq's sister, was amusing baby Aua, who squealed each time Ukpijuak uncovered her face with her hands and said, "Boo!"

"How much longer must we stay here?" Qajaq cried.

"You know we cannot leave until the sewing is finished," Natsiq said gently. "Be patient. The skins will soon be sewn."

Qajaq knew his family would not move from the tundra onto the frozen sea until his mother had finished sewing warm winter caribou clothing for everybody. Caribou were animals of the land, and his people did not believe in preparing their skins on the sea. "Tomorrow?" Qajaq asked hopefully.

His mother smiled at him. Natsiq's teeth were well worn from chewing skins to soften them for sewing. Even then, it was difficult to pull threads of sinew made from animal tendons through the thick fur pelts. Her fingers were worn flat from the work.

"I had to make a completely new outfit for Ukpijuak," she said. "Your sister has grown so this year! Just as you have, Qajaq." Then she turned to Qajaq's sister and handed her a fur parka. "Try this on, Ukpijuak."

Ukpijuak pulled the *amautiq* (ah-MAO-tee) over her head. The hood of the woman's parka was large and there was a pouch on the back. Since she was now twelve years old, Ukpijuak often helped her mother by carrying her baby sister in the pouch. Everybody was delighted with Aua, the little girl they had adopted last spring from Qajaq's aunt and uncle, who had so many little ones to care for.

"But there's nothing to do!" complained Qajaq, as he poked Piujuq, their new puppy, to wake her up.

"Stop buzzing about like a mosquito!" Qajaq's father said at last from where he sat carving a new knife.

Ukpijuak held a small white circle of caribou skin next to the hem of her parka. Then she chose a brown one, diamond-shaped, to see which would make the prettiest decoration. She puckered her lips as she studied each piece. "You won't always be a little pesky mosquito, Qajaq," she said.

Qajaq waited. Sometimes his sister's tongue could sting like a whip.

"Someday," she continued slowly, "you will be a big," her eyes grew wide, "big, pesky mosquito!" She laughed.

Qajaq's cheeks felt warm. He could never think of clever words to spit back at her when she teased him. He thought about her shiny black braids and how, if he gave them a good yank, she would screech like an owl. Instead, he swooped to grab a fistful of the skin scraps she was collecting. He jumped about, holding them overhead. "Look at me! I am Ukpijuak. A big bird! Nya! Nya!"

"Qajaq!" Natsiq pointed to where Maniq sat carving his knife. "Where is the knife you have been learning to carve?"

Maniq interrupted his work and waited. "Bring it over, Qajaq. We will work together."

Ukpijuak wrinkled her nose and sang gaily, "Yes, Qajaq, why don't you?"

Some Inuit called Ukpijuak smart. She could track caribou as cleverly and as quietly as a wolf. Others said she was like a fox that can spot the movement of a tiny lemming at a great distance. Many, including Grandfather, were certain she had inherited the wisdom of her grandmother who, even until her death, could tell from which direction a winter storm would arise or when ice would begin to break from the land in the springtime. Everyone thought Qajaq was lucky to have her for his sister.

Everyone, that is, except Qajaq. He raised his arms to throw the scraps of skin at her.

"Qajaq." Maniq's voice was firm.

Qajaq let the pieces fall, and with a sigh sat beside his father.

"Feel the smooth handle of this knife," said Maniq, holding it close to Qajaq.

Qajaq sat still as he ran his fingers over the surface. It was amazing to see bones and jagged antlers become beautiful tools in his father's skillful hands.

Qajaq worked on his own knife, but the carving tool he used slipped on the surface, making gouges where he did not want them. "I wish I could carve like you, Father," he said.

"Patience, Qajaq."

Piujuq yawned. The puppy had been curled near Maniq's feet, and now was awake and looking for fun. She wiggled her way nearer to Qajaq and licked his fingers. Qajaq could not resist. He somersaulted with the pup, one growling, the other squealing in fun.

"My needle case! Qajaq! Watch where . . ."

But it was too late. Natsiq's ivory needles spilled from the case. Natsiq shook her head and reached to gather them. Her long braided hair fell over the shoulder of her parka.

Ukpijuak covered a smile with her hand. Aua's eyes narrowed as she laughed, and her plump cheeks shone like the snowy owl's eggs Qajaq once found on the tundra.

Grandfather stopped singing. "Ha!" he said. "I no longer hear the wind. This would be a good time to check the trap we built, Qajaq. Maniq, why don't you take the boy to see if we've caught a little fox?"

Maniq laid aside his tools and stretched his arms. "A good idea!" He walked to the tent flap and pushed it aside. "Ah, just a light snow, now." He slipped his outer parka over the one he wore inside the tent. He slung a skin bag with supplies over his shoulder. "Are you ready, Qajaq?"

"Can I go too?" Ukpijuak asked eagerly. Qajaq hoped his father would refuse.

"It would be a good time to train Piujuq to run with the dogs," Maniq said.

"She has not been out for many days," Ukpijuak hastened to add.

Piujuq waited, too, for his answer. Her head was cocked, with her ears perked.

"All right, then," Maniq said. "We will all three go."

Qajaq was not happy. He wanted to be away from Ukpijuak for a while.

4

The Fox Trap

The dogs lifted their heads out of the snow as Maniq, Ukpijuak, and Qajaq left the tent.

Qajaq raced ahead. "Let me do it! I'll fasten them!"

The dogs began to nip at one another. The lead dog stood. She fixed the bickering team with her eyes and bared her teeth. They stopped and waited as Qajaq fastened the sealskin harness.

Maniq grinned and said, mostly to himself, "Ah, Qajaq. You are like a wolf cub--always moving, but not always moving wisely!" He checked the thongs that held the dog traces to the sledge, made a few adjustments, then waited for Qajaq to finish.

"Well done!" he said.

Ukpijuak carried the squirming pup to the sledge. Then she placed her on the ground, holding her beside the other dogs.

Maniq picked up his whip. It was time to push off. "Ay! Ay!" he called to the team.

Ukpijuak and the pup ran in front of Maniq with Qajaq beside them. Qajaq's fur-trimmed hood shielded him from the cold, but the wind stung his cheeks. Flakes of snow stuck on his eyelashes and melted on his tongue. The tundra was quiet, except for the sounds of the wind and the dogs and the fast-moving sledge. Days were short, now, and soon the sun would not appear at all for many days.

In the distance, Qajaq saw movement. What was it? Caribou? Too big to be hares or foxes. As the sledge moved closer, the figures became clearer--two lumbering white bears.

"Polar bears!" Qajaq yelled excitedly. "Watch out, old bears, I will come after you!"

The bears stopped and turned their heads to listen.

"Such brave words from one who has not yet caught more than fish and a few birds," Maniq chided his son.

"Will you take one, Father? You have your weapons, and I will help," Qajaq added boldly.

"Too dangerous, Qajaq!" Maniq said. "That is a cub and its mother. You've never seen the fury of a mother bear protecting her young." Maniq cracked his whip and the dogs sped onward, while the curious bears became dark silhouettes against the pink and purple horizon.

Qajaq looked ahead for the fox trap. He remembered how he and Grandfather had built it, piling stones on top of each other to construct a dome about as tall as Grandfather. When they were finished, it resembled an *igluvigaq* (eeg-LOO-vee-gack), the snow-house they would live in during the winter.

"If you place the rocks this way," Grandfather had explained that day as he angled them gradually, "the fox can easily climb to the roof. Then we'll leave a hole, just large enough for him to jump through to the floor."

"But a fox is smart!" Qajaq had said. "Why would he jump in?" He thought for a moment. "Bait! We'll place some meat inside!" Then he had another thought. "But, Grandfather," he said, "how will the fox know that food is inside?"

Grandfather pulled out a small sealed bag and opened it. "We'll sprinkle this blood on the ground outside and up to the roof. Then, we'll wait. The fox will come . . . in time."

Qajaq smiled, remembering that special time with his grandfather. As Maniq slowed the dogs, Qajaq saw the dome of snow. "There it is!" he shouted and ran faster. "I will see if the fox is inside!"

"Wait, Qajaq!" Maniq ordered. But Qajaq was already there, climbing up the snowy trap to the opening.

Crash!

Snow, ice, and frozen bits of soil collapsed under Qajaq as he tumbled, out of sight, into the trap.

Luckily, Qajaq's thick fur parka cushioned him from the fall. Dazed for a moment, he sat still. Around him was darkness. He smelled a strong, musky odor. Suddenly something brushed past him and more snow tumbled down. Qajaq looked up and saw the swish of a bushy white tail, as it waved and disappeared through the hole his fall had made. Then everything was quiet, except for the sound of Qajaq's pounding heart.

"Qajaq!"

Qajaq saw his father peering down at him. "I'm sorry, Father. I didn't mean to . . ."

Maniq reached in to pull out his son. "Are you hurt?"

"What does it matter?" Qajaq answered glumly. He looked toward his sister, who was giggling. "The fox is gone!"

"No one is born a good hunter, my son. You will learn, just as we all learned." Maniq gave Ukpijuak a meaningful look, as he brushed snow from the seat of Qajaq's trousers. "Come. The three of us will rebuild the trap."

They worked quickly, for it was almost dark, and then Maniq turned the sledge homeward. Only one could be happy at the outcome of this adventure--the little white fox.

Grandfather Tells a Story

Soup, steaming and thick with caribou meat, was ready when Maniq, Ukpijuak, and Qajaq returned to the tent.

Qajaq was not very hungry. He ate a few mouthfuls, then moved close to Grandfather. Grandfather lifted a spoon to his lips and swallowed. His old, clouded eyes studied Qajaq. "You went out today like a herd of thundering caribou and came back like a quiet butterfly. A little tired, I think."

Qajaq leaned his head against the old man's shoulder. "Tell me a story, Grandfather."

Grandfather put an arm around Qajaq. The light from the soapstone lamp Natsiq had lit flickered on the tent walls. Maniq held his new knife toward the flame to examine it closely. Natsiq picked up her needle. Ukpijuak unbraided her hair and began pulling an ivory comb through the long, dark tresses.

The old man said, "I know just the story for you. It's one *my* grandfather told me." He took a long breath and began.

Once there was a village with only two houses. Inside each house there was almost no food, for the hunters had been unable to find game. At last, the people in one of the houses caught a seal. Those who lived in the other house greeted them happily as the hunters returned.

Each family had always shared its catch with the other family, but this time, as the neighbors carried their seal home, they said, "We know it is not the right thing to do, but we are going to keep the whole seal for ourselves."

The other family, disappointed, returned home. The children became too hungry to play or hunt for small animals, and their old grandfather grew so weak that he could not get out of the bed.

The old man's son was still able to search for game. He went hunting earlier and earlier each morning and returned later and later each night.

At last he spied a bear—a giant polar bear. It had made a shelter in the snow, and it lay there with its cubs. The hunter knew that he would need a huge harpoon to kill such a large bear, so he returned to his home to make one.

Qajaq interrupted. "That bear was like the one we saw today. It was so big!" He extended his arms as far as he could reach, as Grandfather continued.

As soon as the large harpoon was made, the hunter went to kill the bear. The old man managed to leave his bed to join his son. When they found the bears' shelter, the son quickly, with all his strength, thrust his harpoon into the bear.

The bear crawled from its lair, growling, as the old man ran toward it. The bear sucked in his breath . . . so deeply that the old man was pulled right down the bear's throat into its belly.

Qajaq sat upright. "Into his belly?"

"Yes, yes!" Grandfather continued.

Fortunately, the old man had his knife and he slit the bear's belly open as fast as he could. His clothes were almost boiled when he fell out of the bear, and the skin on his face was almost scalded. He had nearly suffocated!

The son stabbed the bear over and over with his harpoon until finally the animal lay dead.

The son and his father cut only a small piece of meat from the bear to take home with them, leaving the rest of the large animal in the lair. As they passed the neighbors' house, the old man called loudly. "Neighbors! My son has killed a bear, but we will not give you any gift of meat, not even a scrap for your children."

The father and son shared the meat with their own family. Then gathering their belongings, they all moved to the place where the bear had been killed and built a snowhouse. Now they had meat to last all winter, but the other family--who would not share its seal--starved to death.

Closing his eyes, Grandfather stopped talking and Qajaq leaned closer to him. After a moment Qajaq asked, "How could a bear swallow a man? That really didn't happen, did it? Wouldn't we share our food even if our neighbors wouldn't?

Grandfather had grown weary. "All good questions," he answered with a yawn. "Good questions . . . we'll talk about them tomorrow."

To the Winter Camp

The sledge was piled high, ready for the trip across the frozen strait to their winter camp of Igloolik. Caribou fur bedding, ivory and bone tools, weapons for seal hunting, Natsiq's heavy soapstone lamp--everything the family would need to survive the cold winter was lashed to the sledge. The dogs objected. It took stern shouts from Maniq and cracks of the whip over their heads before they began to pull and strain forward.

Soon the runners were gliding smoothly over the snow. Excitement danced in the crisp air. Her sewing finished, Natsiq was eager to see her sisters' new babies. Maniq's harpoon was ready; he was anxious to taste the ringed seal again. Grandfather took deep breaths of the cold tundra air, as though there would not be many more trips over the frozen desert for him. Ukpijuak raced beside her father, thinking of her friends at camp. Qajaq was happy as he rode on the sledge, with Piujuq snuggled in his lap. He hoped that this would be the year he would hunt his first seal.

They had begun their journey at daybreak but now a curtain of darkness was falling. It was difficult to see beyond the lead dog as Maniq stopped the sledge. "Are we there?" Qajaq asked.

"No, but we have gone as far as we can today," said Maniq. "We'll cross over to Igloolik tomorrow."

Flashes of beautiful color streaked the dark sky, the Northern Lights. After Grandfather and Maniq decided that there wasn't enough good snow for a snowhouse, they set up the tent. Natsiq arranged the bedding and cut portions of dried fish with her *ulu* (OO-loo)--her woman's knife-- for everybody to eat before bedtime. Qajaq barely heard her whisper goodnight to him as he drifted off to sleep.

That night Qajaq had a dream. In the dream, Qajaq was on the ice carrying his harpoon. He was looking, as a hunter would, for holes in the

ice that the seals swimming below use for breathing. The wind was blowing hard, sending up gusts of snow. It was impossible to see, so instead Qajaq listened. Suddenly the wind whispered in his ear, "Here it is, here it is!" And Qajaq looked down to see a glistening mound of snow at his feet. Then ever so slowly the mound disappeared and the dream ended.

In the morning, the family was on its way again. This day's journey would not be long. Soon several snowhouses were outlined against the horizon. Qajaq saw fur-wrapped figures running to greet them.

"Ha! Maniq! Natsiq! Welcome!"

Qajaq was hugged over and over, spun from one pair of arms to another. His nose was pressed by so many other noses that he touched it with his palm to be certain it was still there.

"Qajaq, you have grown!" his aunts and uncles told him. "You look like your father."

At last he was pulled from the crowd by his cousin Amarualik and his friend Ivalu. "Come, see our animals, Qajaq. Bring your bow and arrows, too," they said.

They led him to a clearing and Qajaq saw the snow animals--a polar bear and a caribou. The boys' fathers had carved them from snow so the children could practice being hunters. The snow animals already had holes from the boys' arrows.

Qajaq placed an arrow against his braided sinew bow string. One eye closed, he focused on the bear, remembering the ones he had seen on the way to Grandfather's fox trap. He pulled the arrow back, then *swoosh*, it sped forward--missing the snow bear completely.

"Hah!" Ivalu laughed. "The animals are safe when you're shooting, Qajaq."

"Try again, Qajaq," Amarualik encouraged him, handing him a second arrow. "You just need practice."

Meanwhile, Maniq and Grandfather had found good hard snow for the snowhouse. Grandfather etched a circle on the sea ice where the *igluvigaq* would be built.

Maniq began to cut blocks of the snow. "My new knife works well," he said.

Then the men worked

quickly together. Grandfather pushed the first six blocks into place, and Maniq sliced them with his knife to form a ramp. After they finished the first layer, they placed blocks atop the ramp and added more layers, Gradually, the blocks spiraled upward until the *igluvigaq* took shape.

Natsiq and Ukpijuak worked on the outside, filling in openings between snow blocks with loose snow. Before the top layers were in place, they tossed all the family's belongings inside.

Finally, Maniq cut a door, a window of ice from the lake, and a hole in the roof to allow air to escape. They had worked fast! In about three hours the house was ready to receive them.

Natsiq called Qajaq. "There will be time to enjoy your friends tomorrow night," she said, when he reached the new snowhouse. "Now that everyone has arrived at the winter camp, we will have a reunion at the *qaggiq* (KAH-gerk)." The *qaggiq* was a large snowhouse nearby, big enough to hold all the Inuit at the camp. "But first we must all prepare our house. You can gather ice so I can melt it for our drinking water."

After Qajaq chipped ice from the lake, he crawled through the doorway into the snowhouse. His mother had made their bed on the snow platform. He could see the carefully arranged polar bear and caribou skins. It already felt warm inside. Then Qajaq had a terrible thought! Quickly he turned around and ran outside again.

He snatched the snow beater, made from caribou antler, that was stuck in a snow block outside. Using it, he beat the snow from his clothing-- every white flake. If he did not do this, the snow would melt and then freeze again when he left the snowhouse. How foolish he would feel if he suffered frostbite by forgetting. And what would Ukpijuak have to say about that?

13

Reunion

"Will we go to the *qaggiq* soon?" Qajaq asked. "I saw Amarualik and his family heading over there."

"*Ajurnamat* (ai-YOUR-nah-maat)," answered Natsiq, which in the Inuit language means that waiting is a part of life. She handed a bag to him. "You can carry this arctic char."

Qajaq lifted the bag of dried fish, fish that he had helped to catch with his *kakivak* (KA-kee-vack, fishing spear) last summer. The water was alive with fish then, when the arctic char were leaving the ocean to swim up the rivers to spawn. Though the family had eaten many, there was a good supply remaining for tonight's feasting at the *qaggiq*.

Finally, Qajaq's family joined the others in the big snowhouse. Natsiq took the arctic char from Qajaq and placed the fish on the snow bench with the food others had brought to share. Qajaq helped himself to seal, caribou, some arctic char, and his favorite, *maqtaaq* (MAHK-taak), the sweet skin of the beluga whale. Aua watched him, smacking her lips. Qajaq offered his sweet-tasting finger for her to lick. She rewarded him with a smile. Natsiq, meanwhile, was chewing food to place in the baby's mouth so she could swallow it easily.

All about him people were playing games and talking. Qajaq caught sight of Amarualik and Ivalu sitting on the floor facing one another, the soles of their feet touching. He ran toward them.

Amarualik said, "Want to play *arsuruniq* (ar-SOO-ruh-nirk)?"

Qajaq knelt to watch. Each boy held a piece of antler, joined together by a length of sinew. They pulled hard away from each other, their arms and legs straight, until Ivalu finally gave in. His legs buckled and his body fell forward.

"That's two out of three," announced Amarualik. "I win!"

As they took turns playing *arsuruniq,* Qajaq noticed several girls around Ukpijuak and heard bits of their conversation.

"What a beautiful parka! Where did you find such skins?" The girls touched Ukpijuak's soft fur parka and clasped their hands in delight.

Ukpijuak lowered her eyes and answered softly. "They are from the belly of a caribou that ran past Grandfather and me as we gathered berries. You know how beautiful the skins are late in the summer, new and thick as cold weather comes nearer."

"You mean you shot it, Ukpijuak?" Ilupalik asked. Everyone knew that Grandfather's eyes were too dim to use his bow and arrows. "The tundra was covered with plants that had juicy berries," continued Ukpijuak, without answering the question. "Lemmings were running here and there. I spotted a ground squirrel. He was so funny, sitting on his hind legs, begging for food. I raised my arm to throw some plants to him. But I caught sight of something large, moving while it grazed."

Amarualik and Ivalu were listening now, too. They stopped their game and moved closer to Ukpijuak.

"Did you get the caribou?" Ilupalik asked again.

"I guided Grandfather's hands. It was a lucky shot," Ukpijuak said shyly. "It went down right away."

Qajaq plunked himself down on the floor, away from the group. "A lucky shot," he muttered. It was always Ukpijuak! Smart Ukpijuak! Wonderful Ukpijuak! Qajaq felt like the gray shadow cast by a sunlit tundra flower. Ukpijuak was the flower.

Someone shouted, "The singing is about to begin!" Amarualik and Ivalu returned to Qajaq. Each pulled an arm. "Sit with us, Qajaq. Uncle Qatalik is the first singer."

The center of the *qaggiq* was cleared for the performers. Qatalik stepped forward. In his left hand, he held a drum made from a walrus bladder stretched over a wooden frame. In his right, he held a short stick. The audience was silent as he spoke.

"I may not remember my songs and they are not very important," he said humbly. Then the drum rumbled. As Qatalik played, he swayed from side to side, in rhythm with the drum beats.

"Why are his eyes closed?" Amarualik whispered to Qajaq.

"So he can see into his thoughts," Qajaq replied. "That's what Grandfather says."

Qatalik's song was about a hunter in search of walrus. It told how the hunter was able to overpower the animal because of his amulet, a good luck piece that was sewn in his parka. Qatalik's song lasted for a very long time. He sang parts of it over and over again.

15

I could not sleep
For the sea was so smooth
Near at hand.
So I rowed out
And up came a walrus
Close by my kayak.
It was too near to throw,
So I thrust my harpoon into its side
And the bladder-float danced across
        the waves.
But in a moment it was up again,
Setting its flippers angrily
Like elbows on the surface of the water
And trying to rip up the bladder.
All in vain it wasted its strength,
For the skin of an unborn lemming
Was sewn inside as an amulet to guard.
Then snorting viciously it sought to
        gather strength,
But I rowed up
And ended the struggle.
Hear that, O men from strange creeks and fiords
That were always so ready to praise yourselves;
Now you can fill your lungs with song
Of another man's bold hunting.

Qajaq thought of his dream about the seal hunt. He hoped that tomorrow he, too, would be successful.

Later that night, Qajaq watched Natsiq tuck Aua next to him under the fur blanket. She rubbed her nose gently over the baby's tiny one. Maniq came in and removed his outer parka.

"Can I hunt with you tomorrow, Father?" Qajaq asked.

"We'll see in the morning," said Maniq.

He's afraid I'll scare the seal away like I scared the fox, thought Qajaq. He sighed deeply and buried himself beneath the fur.

"It may be a long wait at the breathing hole . . . a long time for a boy to be very quiet," Maniq warned. He placed his wet mittens on the drying rack over the soapstone lamp.

Qajaq sat upright. "I can be very quiet," he said in a small voice, trying to sound convincing.

Grandfather pulled an object he had been carving from his pile of

belongings. "I have something for you," he said to Qajaq. "Every hunter needs an amulet for good luck." He opened his hand, and Qajaq saw a small seal, carved of ivory.

"Its claws and eyes look so real, Grandfather!" Qajaq eagerly reached to touch it. "And it's so smooth!"

"The spirit of the seal is in this amulet," said Grandfather. "Treat it with respect." He gently placed the carving in his grandson's hand.

Later that night under the thick caribou blanket, Qajaq lay wide awake. He clutched his amulet as he listened to the breathing of his sleeping family, everyone together on the platform. Father's was the loudest, almost a snore, and baby Aua's sounded like quick, tiny sighs. He heard a yawn escape from Natsiq's lips, and felt the caribou skin move as she leaned toward the lamp to adjust the flame. Then Qajaq, too, fell asleep. And as he slept, he dreamed once more of the hunt.

The Seal Hunt

"If you are coming with me, hurry," Maniq called. "The days are short. We must make the most of the light."

"I'm coming, Father!" Qajaq answered. He fidgeted while Natsiq stitched his ivory seal to the inside of his parka.

Ukpijuak had hitched the dogs, and Maniq was waiting to crack the whip when Qajaq hopped onto the sledge. The three of them traveled a few miles before seeing the other hunters, already waiting at their breathing holes.

"Do you want to stay with me, Qajaq?" Maniq asked. "You might not find a breathing hole of your own."

"No," said Qajaq, jumping from the sledge. "I'll look over there." He pointed beyond a few hunters, not sure why he had decided on that direction.

"Look for the small mounds of snow," Maniq called as Qajaq moved on. "The holes are buried beneath them."

"I know!" Qajaq said, thinking of his dream.

Maniq laughed. "How much my young hunter knows already!"

Qajaq walked far and long in his search for a breathing hole. Swirls of snow blinded him at times. The wind seemed to lift him in its gusts. Then he saw it . . . a mound as close as the length of his harpoon, just as he had seen in his dream. Qajaq pushed the snow from the breathing hole with the blunt end of his harpoon. Then he used a long, curved piece of antler to find the angle of the tunnel underneath. He pushed it in slowly, studying its movement. He remembered Maniq's words: "This will show you which way the seal will rise. Then you'll know how to aim your harpoon."

Qajaq cut a block of snow with his knife and set it nearby to block the hole from the wind. Next, he positioned a stiff sinew string attached to a feather that would flutter when the seal breathed at the hole. Qajaq stood upon his caribou bag. The bag protected his feet from the cold and cushioned them so the ice beneath would not creak, alerting the seal. Then he waited.

And he waited.

He knew he had never stood so long, so quietly. He knew he had never felt so cold. Qajaq tucked his mittened hands into his sleeves and tried to grasp his arms. He wiggled his fingers. Could he still feel them? They tingled. He felt the amulet Grandfather had given him. The thought of his grandfather's kind face cheered him a little, and he tried to smile.

He waited longer. The sky turned a dusky gray. Still the wind. Still the blowing snow. Qajaq blinked back tears. "I've waited," he said in despair. "I have been patient. Will I never have my chance?" The wind howled in answer. Qajaq closed his eyes.

When he opened them again, he saw a figure against the darkening horizon. He blinked. The figure was moving toward him--dogs, a sledge, a waving arm. It was Ukpijuak! She came quickly now, circling around him.

What is she doing? he wondered. Then, watching her, he knew. She was frightening the seals at the surrounding breathing holes, so they would swim to his!

Qajaq grabbed his harpoon, his eyes glued to the feather. Ukpijuak drove the dogs around and around. Suddenly the feather fluttered, and Qajaq heard the seal breathing. He thrust the harpoon and felt it strike.

"I have it! I've caught my seal!" he yelled.

Ukpijuak jumped from the sledge and came running. "Hold it tight," she called. Soon she was kneeling beside him, widening the opening with the harpoon's shaft. Qajaq clutched the harpoon's line.

Ukpijuak settled back on her heels. "The hole is large enough now. Can you pull it through?" she asked.

"Of course!"

Qajaq answered quickly. He stood. He pulled. He slid toward the hole. Although ringed seals are the smallest of seals, it is not easy to pull them from the sea.

"The men often help one another," Ukpijuak said. "If you want, I can tug, too."

Qajaq did not want to lose his seal, so he let Ukpijuak grip the line. Together they slowly eased the dead seal from the hole. Then they fell down next to it, panting.

When he had caught his breath, Qajaq reached into his caribou bag and removed a knife. He cut a small hole in the seal, as he had seen his father do, just large enough to remove the liver and a little blubber. He cut pieces of each for Ukpijuak. Nothing helped cold hunters quite as much as warm meat from the seal. It was the custom to share it, but since this was Qajaq's first seal, he would not eat from it. This, too, was a custom.

Just then Maniq appeared to announce that it was time to go home. "A seal! Is it yours, Ukpijuak?" he asked with raised eyebrows.

Ukpijuak shook her head.

"Qajaq!" Maniq shouted. He pounded Qajaq soundly on the back. "My little hunter! You must give it a drink of fresh water."

Qajaq looked up at his father and smiled, no longer feeling the cold. He pulled his waterbag from under his parka and knelt by the seal. Gently he poured the fresh water over the seal's mouth. He watched quietly as the glistening droplets trickled from the seal onto the snow.

It was customary for the hunter to offer fresh water to the dead seal, because the Inuit believed that seals swim in the salt water, always searching for fresh water. If the hunter pleased the seal's spirit in this way, it would provide more seals for him in future hunts.

As Qajaq rose to his feet, he looked shyly at his sister. "I would not have caught the seal without your help," he admitted, finally feeling lucky to have a sister like Ukpijuak.

"Now we must hurry home to show Natsiq and Grandfather," Maniq shouted jovially. He looked proudly at both children as he helped them load the seal onto the sledge.

Hearing the returning hunters' shouts, Natsiq ran out to greet them. One look at Qajaq told her whose seal it was, and she too pounded him on the back.

Together, Natsiq and Qajaq gathered clean snow to spread on the floor of the *igluvigaq.* Clean snow would honor the seal.

After Maniq dragged the seal inside, he bent beside it and cut away parts of its body. Qajaq sat cross-legged nearby, watching his father's skillful motions. He held the puppy, who tried to snatch pieces of the meat. "You will have your dinner with the other dogs," he laughed.

When his job was finished, Maniq put his knife aside. "Now, Qajaq. Your seal is ready--flippers, liver, blubber, and all the rest of it. Now you can share with our neighbors."

Qajaq stood and picked up portions of the seal. Looking at Ukpijuak, he said, "Will you come with me, Sister?"

Ukpijuak stopped bouncing Aua on her lap and turned toward him. She knew it was a special time for the hunter. Everyone would be pleased to receive a portion from the hunt. But would they smile quite so much upon Qajaq if she were with him?

She tossed her head and looked away from him. "Poor Qajaq. Is the meat too heavy to carry all by yourself?"

Qajaq studied her with a puzzled expression, then shrugged his shoulders and turned to leave. But as he left, he heard her call softly, "Goodbye, little Brother."

Qajaq walked into the night. Everything seemed quiet after the excitement of the day. He thought of the sea beneath him and all the living things swimming in it. He thought of the land his family had left and would return to, alive with caribou and hares and birds and lemmings. How many winters would pass before he would understand each creature's special place on earth? How many springs till he'd know how to use each animal wisely?

The wind stirred. There was much that he did not yet understand, but for the first time he knew he was part of it all. Qajaq felt the wind at his back, and as it pushed him along, he sang:

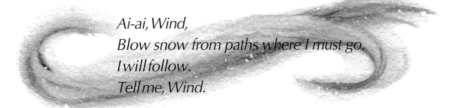

Ai-ai, Wind,
Blow snow from paths where I must go.
I will follow.
Tell me, Wind.

The Land Where Qajaq Lived

Believe it or not, the Arctic is a desert--a frozen, treeless desert! It's a desert because it gets very little rain or snow. In the winter it is so cold in the Arctic that the snow that does fall doesn't melt. So deep snow covers the land. Even the salty oceans and bays freeze. Many of the pictures in this book will give you an idea of how the Canadian Arctic looks in the wintertime.

In summer a frozen layer of earth, called permafrost, remains below the surface of the ground. Water can't drain through this layer of frozen soil, so the ground above is often soggy and small ponds appear.

During the summer you'll find many flowers and other plants that grow close to the ground for protection from the winds. The tallest shrubs are less than a foot (0.3 m) high. Look at the picture on page 34.

Why So Cold in the Arctic?

It is hot at the Equator because the sun's rays hit the land almost directly. Because the Earth is a sphere and is tilted in relation to the sun, the sun's rays strike the Arctic and Antarctica at an angle. These rays are not nearly as strong as direct ones. This drawing gives you an idea of how the rays of the sun hit the Arctic in summer.

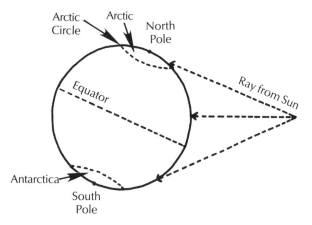

You can perform an experiment to help you understand why it is so cold in the Arctic.

Materials

two tin can lids
dull black poster paint
paintbrush

black electrical tape
modeling clay
lamp with lightbulb

1. Paint the tin can lids black and wrap the sharp edges with the tape.

2. Balls of clay serve as stands. Push the lids into the clay so that one faces the lightbulb directly and the other will receive the light at an angle. Then turn on the lamp.

3. After ten to twenty minutes, test the lids' heat on the inside of your arm. Which is hotter?

Now ask yourself these questions:
- Which lid represents the sun's rays on the Arctic? How does this explain why the Arctic is so cold? (See page 60 for the answer.)
- How does the angle affect the amount of light each lid receives?

the Arctic. The area north of the Arctic Circle.
tundra. The treeless desert (plains) of the arctic region.

Weather Forecast

If you were to spend a year in Igloolik, you might find the following temperatures:

June 21	36° Fahrenheit (2° Celsius)
September 23	34° Fahrenheit (-1° Celsius)
December 21	0° Fahrenheit (-18° Celsius)
March 21	-9° Fahrenheit (-23° Celsius)

Use a red marker or crayon to indicate on the first row of thermometers the temperatures you might find where Qajaq lived. Each thermometer has a Fahrenheit (F) and a Celsius (C) scale. Use the scale you are familiar with.

Then mark the temperatures you might find where you live. Where is it warmer?

The Temperatures in Igloolik

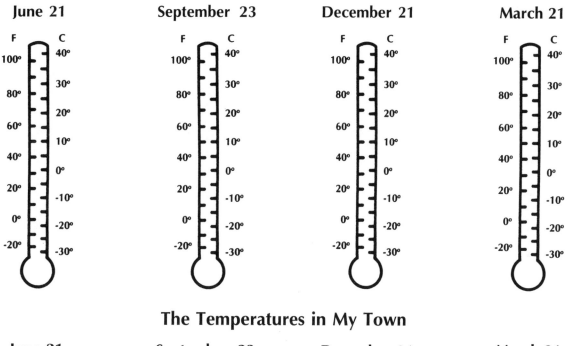

The Temperatures in My Town

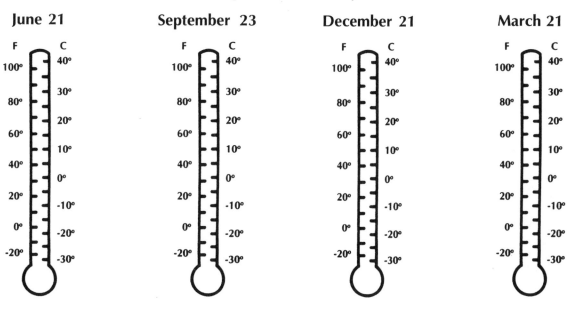

Where's the Sun?

Every year on the *summer solstice,* June 21, there is constant light north of the Arctic Circle. The sun never sets! Each day after June 21 has a little less light than the day before. By the *winter solstice,* December 21, there is constant darkness, when the sun never rises! Each day after December 21 has a little more light than the day before, and by June 21 there is constant light again. Every year on the *spring* and *autumn equinoxes,* March 21 and September 23, the days and nights are of equal length--each has twelve hours.

At Igloolik, where Qajaq lived, the sun is *above* the horizon for sixty-six days from May 19 to July 24. The sun is *below* the horizon from November 29 to January 15. Here's when it is light in Igloolik at the solstices and equinoxes:

June 21: daylight for twenty-four hours
September 23: daylight from 7:05 am to 7:20 pm
December 21: twilight from 11 am to 1:30 pm
March 21: daylight from 6:05 am to 6:20 pm

Show when it is dark and light in Igloolik by coloring the top four circles. Use a black marker or crayon to indicate darkness and a yellow one for daylight. Use both colors for twilight.

Now color the bottom four circles in the same way to show what parts of the day are dark and light where you live. Are the days shorter in summer or winter where you live?

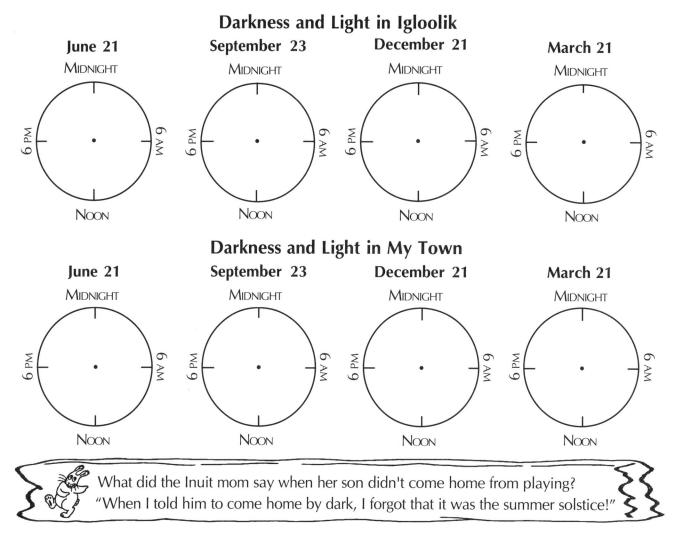

Darkness and Light in Igloolik

June 21   **September 23**   **December 21**   **March 21**

Darkness and Light in My Town

June 21   **September 23**   **December 21**   **March 21**

What did the Inuit mom say when her son didn't come home from playing?
"When I told him to come home by dark, I forgot that it was the summer solstice!"

The Animals Qajaq Knew

Qajaq knew about the animals described below. The Inuit *had* to know.
Their survival in the frozen north depended on the animals they hunted.

Break the Survival Codes

Just like humans, arctic animals must develop special ways of surviving in the harsh cold. These special traits are called adaptations. Through the years each type of animal has developed its own methods of coping with the cold and finding food in winter.

Below you will find three sections about land mammals, sea mammals, and birds. Each section begins with a list of survival codes that help some or all of these animals to survive.

Here's what to do to break the codes:
- Study the survival codes of land mammals.
- Next look at the symbols with each of the land mammals in that section. Without looking back at the codes, try to break each animal's survival codes by writing what the codes mean in the spaces provided. The first animal's codes are done for you. (You can abbreviate the codes.)
- Then break the codes for the sea mammals and birds.

Survival Codes of Land Mammals

 HAS LONG, THICK, WATERPROOF FUR ON ITS BODY. *(This keeps animal warm.)*

 HAS THICK, FURRY HAIR ON ITS FEET (EVEN ON SOLES). *(This provides warmth and acts as snowshoes.)*

 HAS SMALL EARS (E); SHORT, STUBBY TAIL (T); AND/OR SHORT LEGS (L). *(This conserves heat. Imagine how much more energy would be needed to keep long ears, tails, and legs warm!) Pay attention to the three letters in this code.*

 EATS LARGE AMOUNTS OF FOOD IN AUTUMN. *(The body uses food to produce fat for warmth and as stored energy.)*

 STORES FOOD IN AUTUMN FOR WINTER OR SPRING. *(This provides enough food to survive the winter.)*

 BUILDS DEN IN SNOW OR ROCKS. *(This protects animal from cold while it is resting.)*

○ **SPENDS WINTER IN NEST UNDER SNOW OR UNDERGROUND.** *(The temperature is warmer under snow.)*

 HAS SHARP CLAWS ON ITS FOREPAWS. *(These help animal to burrow in snow or dig for food.)*

 HIBERNATES (SPENDS WINTER IN A SLEEP-LIKE STATE). *(This conserves energy.)*

 HAS GRAY OR BROWN FUR IN SUMMER AND WHITE FUR IN WINTER. *(This camouflage helps hide predators and prey. See definitions on page 30.)*

 MIGRATES WITHIN THE ARCTIC IN WINTER. *(This provides food.) See definition of "migrate" on page 29.*

Land Mammals

COLLARED LEMMING

Very small herbivore; grayish-brown in summer, white in winter.

Fascinating Fact. Curiously, every three or four years the lemming population increases dramatically. Then over the next three or four years, the number of lemmings decreases drastically. How do these changes in their population affect many other animals? (See page 60 for the answer.)

Survival Code Thick fur; short Ears, Tail, and Legs; winters under snow; sharp claws; changes color

ERMINE

Very small carnivore; brown in summer, snowy white in winter.

Fascinating Facts. This noisy animal hisses, screeches, chatters, and purrs. In the winter the tip of its tail is black.

Survival Code _____

_____

ARCTIC GROUND SQUIRREL

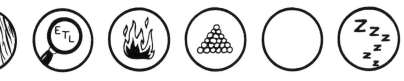

Small brown herbivore.

Fascinating Fact: The Inuit call this animal *siksik* (SICK-sick).

Survival Code ————————————————

———————————————————————

carnivore. An animal that eats only meat.

herbivore. An animal that eats only plants.

omnivore. An animal that eats both meat and plants.

ARCTIC HARE

Medium-sized herbivore. In the far north the arctic hare is white all year round. In the rest of the Arctic its summer coat is gray or brown.

Fascinating Facts. The tips of this animal's ears are sometimes black. Newborn arctic hares can run soon after they are born.

Survival Code _____

_____

ARCTIC FOX

Medium-sized omnivore; grayish brown in summer, white in winter. Some are bluish-gray in winter.

Fascinating Facts. These adventurous foxes travel far and wide on their hunting trips. They often follow large predators, especially polar bears, so they can eat scraps of food the other animals leave behind.

Survival Code _____

_____

GRAY WOLF

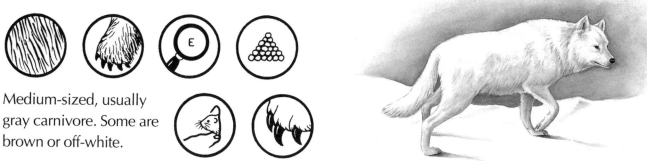

Medium-sized, usually gray carnivore. Some are brown or off-white.

Fascinating Facts. The gray wolf is the largest member of the dog family. Wolves communicate by howling. When they run together in packs, they can kill animals like caribou that weigh ten times more than themselves.

Survival Code _____

CARIBOU

Large tan herbivore.

Fascinating Facts. Caribou, also called reindeer, have the widest feet of all deer. Can you guess why? (See answer on page 60.) Sometimes thousands of caribou travel together.

Survival Code _____

MUSK-OX

Very large, dark brown herbivore.

Fascinating Facts. This animal's hair may be 2 feet (.61 m) long. When wolves attack a herd of musk-oxen, the adults form a circle, facing outward, around their young and weak members. Then strong males dart forward to ward off the predators. (See page 33.)

Survival Code _____

POLAR BEAR

Very large omnivore, although it eats mostly meat; yellowish-white in summer, pure white in winter.

Fascinating Facts. This animal has webbed feet and swims easily. It weighs up to 1,760 pounds (798 kg) and runs up to 18 miles (29 km) an hour. Polar bears do not hibernate in winter.

Survival Code _____

Survival Codes of Sea Mammals

 HAS OILY, WATERPROOF SKIN. *(Oil glands in skin prevent water from entering it.)*

 HAS THICK LAYER OF FAT, CALLED BLUBBER, UNDER SKIN. *(This provides warmth.)*

 HAS THIN FUR COAT. *(This provides some warmth.)*

 HAS SHARP CLAWS ON ITS FRONT FLIPPERS. *(These help animal to make breathing holes in ice.)*

MIGRATES WITHIN THE ARCTIC IN WINTER. *(This avoids frozen water and provides food.) See definition below.*

Sea Mammals

RINGED SEAL

Medium-sized carnivore. Has brown to bluish-black back with cream-colored rings that have dark centers. Its belly is silver.

Fascinating Facts. The smallest of the seal family, the ringed seal has a layer of blubber that is 40 percent of its body weight. Newborn seals have white fur.

Survival Code _____

NARWHAL

Large bluish-gray carnivore.

Fascinating Facts. The Inuit sometimes made a harpoon from the male's ivory tusk. The male narwhal can weigh twice as much as the female.

Survival Code _____

 migrate. To move from one place to another as the seasons change. Animals often migrate to a warmer climate during the cold season, returning when the weather warms.

WALRUS

Very large gray or cinnamon-colored carnivore.

Fascinating Facts. The larger a walrus's tusks the greater its status in its walrus community. Walrus also use their tusks as ice choppers and weapons. They use their sensitive whiskers to find food on the dark sea bottom.

Survival Code _____

BELUGA WHALE

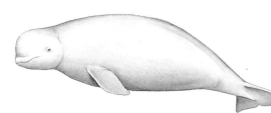

Very large white carnivore.

Fascinating Facts. This animal uses its flexible lips to suck prey off the sea bottom. Because the beluga screams, moos, and trills, whalers nick-named it "sea canary." Belugas usually are found in small groups, except when they migrate. Then several hundred of them might travel together.

Survival Code _____

BOWHEAD WHALE

Huge black or bluish-gray carnivore.

Fascinating Facts. This whale provided the Inuit with large amounts of oil. It is a slow swimmer and floats, rather than sinks, when it is killed, making it easier to catch than some species. Today it is endangered.

Survival Code _____

predator. An animal that catches other animals for food.

prey. An animal that is caught by other animals for food.

Survival Codes of Birds

 HAS LOTS OF FEATHERS. *(Feathers trap air, which serves as insulation.)*

 HAS MANY FEATHERS ON ITS FEET AND ANKLES. *(These provide warmth and act as snowshoes.)*

 BURROWS INTO SNOWBANKS. *(This keeps animal warmer.)*

 HAS BROWN FEATHERS IN SUMMER AND WHITE FEATHERS IN WINTER. *(This camouflage helps both predators and prey.)*

 MIGRATES SOUTH IN WINTER. *(This avoids cold and provides food.) See definition on page 29.*

 EATS LARGE AMOUNTS OF FOOD IN AUTUMN. *(The body uses food to produce heavy fat and energy to migrate.)*

Birds

WILLOW PTARMIGAN

Medium-sized omnivore, although it usually eats plants; mostly brown in summer and white in winter.

Fascinating Facts. The feathers on this bird's feet help it to shuffle through the snow, and it spends a good deal of time on the ground. During winter it flies into snowbanks to sleep at night. The Inuit used this bird's wings in the summertime as feather dusters.

Survival Code _____

_____

SNOWY OWL

Large, primarily white carnivore.

Fascinating Fact. Snowy owls remain on the tundra unless lemmings are scarce. Then they fly southward to find food.

Survival Code _____

_____

SNOW GOOSE

Large herbivore; sometimes white, sometimes dark gray.

Fascinating Facts. Snow Geese come in two colors--all white or dark gray with white heads. Many families of snow geese include both colors. Sometimes these birds have orange heads when they fly south because of the large quantity of iron in arctic waters. When the birds reach under water for aquatic plants, the iron dyes the feathers on their heads orange.

Survival Code _____

Other Arctic Animals

There are many other mammals and birds in the Arctic. Land mammals include the arctic shrew, wolverine, and grizzly bear. Among the mammals in the sea are the bearded seal, harbor seal, and killer whale. Arctic birds include loons, ravens, the snow bunting, tundra swan, arctic tern, and peregrine falcon. Look these up in an encyclopedia to learn about them. How many other arctic animals can you find?

The seas are rich with fish that include polar cod. In the autumn arctic char swim from the oceans to the rivers to lay their eggs. Lake trout and white fish are common freshwater fish.

As soon as winter ends, black flies, mosquitoes, and other insects become a great nuisance to arctic people and animals alike. The warble fly even lays its eggs on the caribou's hair. (Many insects throughout the world hide their eggs in mammals' hair.)

POLAR COD

ARCTIC CHAR

No matter how hard you look, you won't find penguins in the Arctic. These interesting birds live mostly in Antarctica at the opposite end of the Earth.

You won't find snakes, other reptiles, or amphibians either. Their body temperatures depend on the temperature around them, and it's just too cold in the Arctic.

Where, Oh Where, Are the Animals?

In the Wintertime

White fur or feathers often help arctic animals to hide if they are hunting or being hunted. Find the camouflaged polar bear, arctic fox, arctic hare, ermine, snowy owl, and willow ptarmigan. There are *three* hidden lemmings. Then color the picture, but don't color the animals that are white in winter.

Can you name the four animals that *always* change the color of their coats in summer? (See page 60 for the answer.)

In the Summertime

Find the arctic fox, arctic ground squirrel, caribou, ermine, arctic hare, willow ptarmigan, snowy owl, and three lemmings. (Use pages 25-32 to help in identifying them.) Of course, it is unlikely that all these animals would be in the same place at the same time. Color all the animals shades of brown, except the caribou, which is tan, and the snowy owl, which is white all year round. Page 27 will tell you why you could also leave the arctic hare white. Try to camouflage the animals by making them fade into their surroundings.

The Arctic Food Web

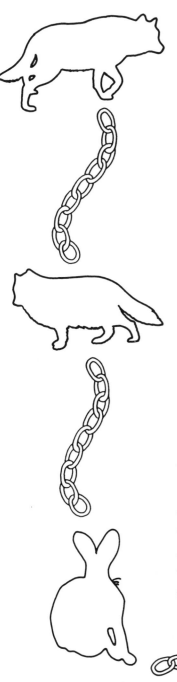

Plants are the foundation of life. If all the plants were to die, all the herbivores (animals that eat only plants) would also die. If there were no herbivores, then the carnivores (animals that eat herbivores) could not live--and *all* life would end! This is true throughout the world, not just in the Arctic.

Food chains show us which animals eat which foods. One arctic chain goes like this: The arctic hare, willow ptarmigan, and lemmings eat various kinds of plants. The arctic fox, a carnivore, preys on the arctic hare, willow ptarmigan, and lemming. The wolf, also a carnivore, sometimes eats the arctic fox. The wolf has no enemies except humans.

There are many other food chains in the Arctic, and some are very complicated. Together these food chains make up the arctic food web.

In all food chains there are more plants than herbivores, and there are more herbivores than carnivores. Usually, this makes it possible for many kinds of animals to survive.

Some years, however, meat eaters have difficulty finding enough food. Perhaps there are fewer lemmings than the year before. Then the number of animals that depend on lemmings will be less too. (See "Collared Lemming" on page 26.) When some animals like the snowy owl cannot find an adequate food supply in the Arctic, they migrate south until they find enough food.

Missing Links

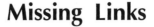

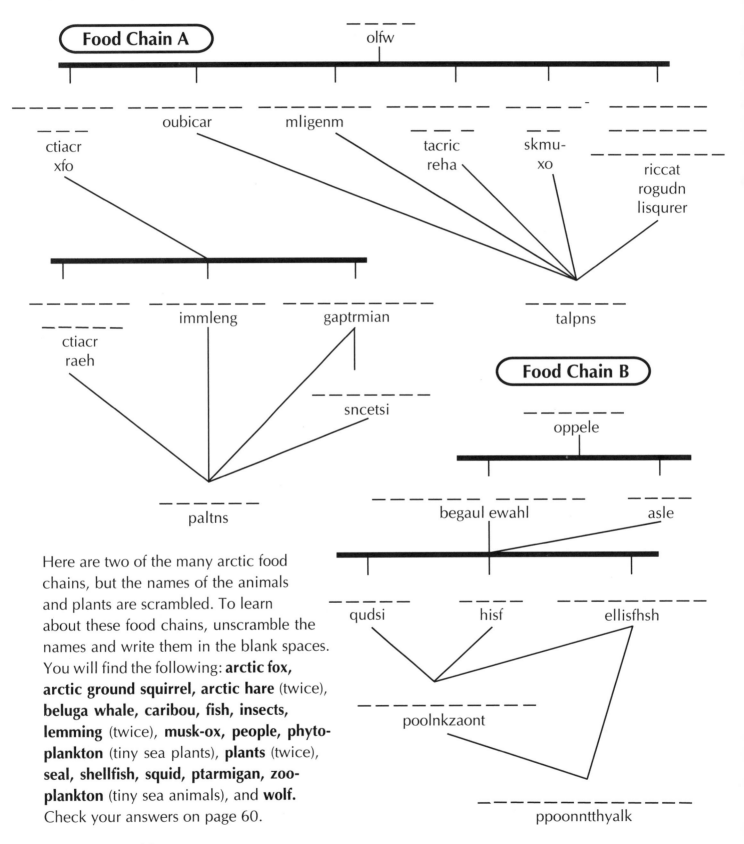

Food Chain A

_ _ _ _
olfw

_ _ _ _ _ _ _
oubicar

_ _ _ _ _ _ _
mligenm

_ _ _
ctiacr
xfo

_ _ _ _ _ _
tacric
reha

_ _ _ _
skmu-
xo

_ _ _ _ _ _
riccat
rogudn
lisqurer

_ _ _ _ _ _ _
immleng

_ _ _ _ _ _ _ _
gaptrmian

_ _ _ _ _ _
talpns

_ _ _ _ _
ctiacr
raeh

_ _ _ _ _ _
sncetsi

Food Chain B

_ _ _ _ _
oppele

_ _ _ _ _
paltns

_ _ _ _ _ _ _ _ _
begaul ewahl

_ _ _
asle

_ _ _ _
qudsi

_ _ _
hisf

_ _ _ _ _ _ _
ellisfhsh

_ _ _ _ _ _ _ _
poolnkzaont

_ _ _ _ _ _ _ _ _ _
ppoonntthyalk

Here are two of the many arctic food chains, but the names of the animals and plants are scrambled. To learn about these food chains, unscramble the names and write them in the blank spaces. You will find the following: **arctic fox, arctic ground squirrel, arctic hare** (twice), **beluga whale, caribou, fish, insects, lemming** (twice), **musk-ox, people, phytoplankton** (tiny sea plants), **plants** (twice), **seal, shellfish, squid, ptarmigan, zooplankton** (tiny sea animals), and **wolf.** Check your answers on page 60.

Arctic Food Chain Mobile

You will need to do "Missing Links" on page 36 before you make your mobile. Be sure to check your answers on page 60.

Materials

compass (or round object like a glass)	transparent tape (optional)
heavy paper	hole punch
pencil	thin string or yarn
crayons or markers	wire coat hanger
scissors	4 plastic straws or sticks

Directions

1. Use the compass or other object to draw 21 circles on the paper. See the illustration for the approximate size. (Don't cut them out yet.)

2. Remove the animal silhouettes below and on page 39 by cutting on the dash lines.

3. Using a windowpane for light, trace an animal or plant in each circle. (You will be tracing some silhouettes twice.)

4. Finish drawing the animals and plants in the silhouettes, color them, and cut out the circles. Write the name of each animal and plant on the back of its circle *as you cut it out.*

5. Use the punch to make holes for the strings. (You may want to reinforce the holes with transparent tape *before* you use the punch.)

6. Using "Missing Links" and the drawing on page 38, arrange the circles into the correct food chains by laying them on a flat surface.

7. Assemble Food Chain A as follows:

● Tie a short piece of string (or yarn) to the hanger and to the top hole of the wolf.

● Tie a short piece of string to the bottom hole of the wolf and to the middle of a straw.

● Tie six strings to the straw and to the top holes of the correct animals.

● Continue this procedure following the food chain diagrams.

● When more than one animal preys on the same thing, make their strings longer. Feed all the strings into the top hole of the prey's circle, and tie them in a knot together.

8. Assemble Food Chain B in the same way.

9. Hang your mobile and move the strings around on the straws until it is balanced.

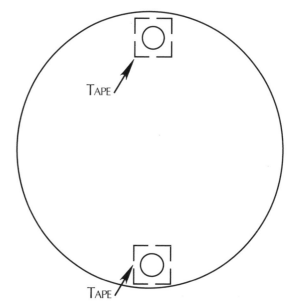

TAPE

TAPE

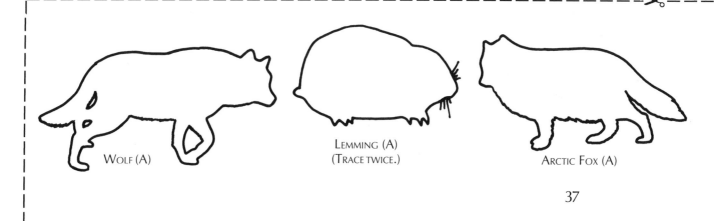

WOLF (A)

LEMMING (A)
(TRACE TWICE.)

ARCTIC FOX (A)

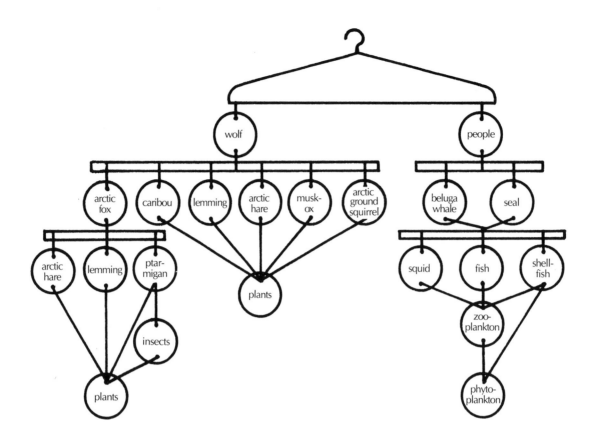

Bonus Food Chain

Here is a third arctic food chain that you can add to your mobile if you're really energetic. It takes ten circles. Most of the silhouettes you will need are on pages 37 and 39. You will find snowy owl and ermine silhouettes on page 35. You can draw your own birds' eggs. Hang this food chain from the hanger between the other two chains.

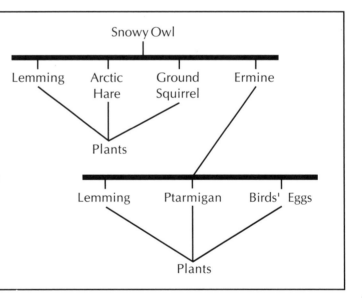

CARIBOU (A)

INSECTS (A)

SEAL (A)

PEOPLE (B)

MUSK-OX (A)

PLANTS (A)
(TRACE TWICE.)

BELUGA WHALE (A)

PTARMIGAN (A)

SHELLFISH (B)

FISH (B)

SQUID (B)

ARCTIC GROUND
SQUIRREL (A)

ARCTIC HARE (A)
(TRACE TWICE.)

ZOOPLANKTON (B)

PHYTOPLANKTON (B)

Create an Arctic Animal

Design your own imaginary arctic animal. First, plan your animal by answering these questions.

How will it protect itself from the cold? _____

How will it protect itself from other animals? _____

What color will it be? _____

What will it eat and how will it get its food? _____

Where will it sleep? _____

What is its name? _____

When you are sure that it has everything it needs to survive, draw it on this page.

Hunting to Survive

In order to survive, the Inuit hunted many kinds of animals. They used various parts of the animals for food, clothing, tools, summer tents, and other items, including children's toys. They wasted very little of their catch and did not hunt for sport.

WALRUS HUNTING WAS A DANGEROUS SUMMER ACTIVITY. SEVERAL MEN, EACH IN A KAYAK, WORKED TOGETHER USING HARPOONS ATTACHED TO SEALSKIN FLOATS. AFTER THE HARPOON ENTERED THE WALRUS, THE SEALSKIN FLOAT SLOWED THE ANIMAL AS IT TRIED TO ESCAPE. THE FLOAT ALSO MADE IT POSSIBLE TO LOCATE THE WALRUS. (NOTE THE FLOAT BEHIND THE HUNTER.)

Lower the Light

During the spring, the Inuit could be temporarily blinded from the glare of the sun on the white snow. They wore snow goggles on hunting trips and at other times to protect their eyes. The goggles were often made from ivory and had small slits that let in only a little light.

To make your own snow goggles, you will need the following materials:

paper	pencil	hole punch
lightweight cardboard	scissors	string

First, use the paper to trace these snow goggles. Make a pattern by cutting out the paper goggles. Then trace the pattern onto cardboard, and cut out the cardboard goggles. (You may need help with the slits.) Punch out the two holes, and tie a length of string in each hole.

Now you're ready to face the arctic glare. Just tie your snow goggles in place.

BONUS: Why didn't the Inuit need goggles in the middle of winter? (See page 60.)

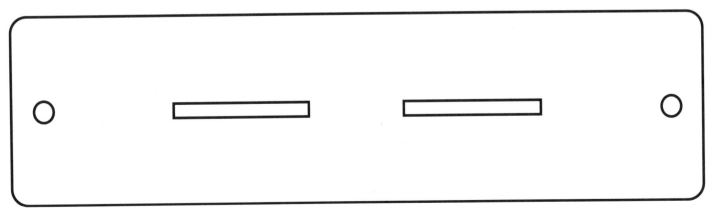

The Inuit Way

Qajaq's grandfather made him a charm called an amulet. His mother sewed the amulet into his parka so it would be close to him while he was hunting seals.

Inuit hunters often wore amulets. They believed that these charms would aid them in the hunt. Sometimes they carved ivory animals from a walrus tusk. Other amulets were simply objects from the natural world like feathers or animal skins.

Here's how to make an amulet.

POLAR BEAR AMULET

WHALE AMULET

Materials
bar of Ivory soap
butter knife or plastic knife
large masonry nail

1. Decide whether you want to "hunt" a whale or a polar bear.

2. Use the knife to scrape off the lettering from half a cake of soap. With the nail lightly draw the animal's silhouette. Then draw the animal in reverse on the other side of the soap.

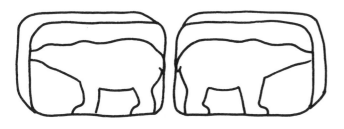

3. With the knife carefully carve away the soap a little at a time until you have only the animal's basic shape left. Continue to work, smoothing and rounding the edges, until you are satisfied with the way it looks.

4. Use the nail to engrave the fine details (such as eyes, fur, and claws).

5. Allow your amulet to dry out for a couple of days. Then polish it by carefully rubbing it with a paper napkin.

6. Find an old shirt and sew your amulet into its hem.

Now you are ready for the hunt! Imagine how you could use this animal if you lived in the Arctic.

Polar bears dig dens in the snow. The female gives birth in the den and keeps her cubs safely inside until they are old enough to accompany her on hunting trips. Male bears sometimes seek protection in dens, too.

What a snug, cozy place to wait out the storm! Do you think anyone lives here?

Used Parts

Can you picture an Inuit picking bits of food from his teeth with a walrus-whisker toothpick or a mother bandaging her son's injured arm with a lemming skin? Imagine what blood soup would taste like. Throughout this book you can read about the kinds of things the Inuit used to survive in the Arctic. This activity will help you discover what animal parts the Inuit used for some of these items. Begin with page 45. Follow each line from an animal part until you reach how it was used. (You can trace the lines with colored markers.) As you discover how a part was used, write it under the correct heading on this page.

Skin

Meat

Sinew

Bone

Blubber

Ivory

Antlers

Blood

Bird's Wing

Ajajaq(toy)
Amulets
Bait
Blankets
Bow Strings
Boat Coverings
Combs
Dog Food
Food
Harpoons
Knives
Needles
Oil
Parkas
Seal Probes
Snow Beaters
Snow Goggles
Tents
Thread

ANIMAL PARTS

Skin
Bone
Ivory
Meat
Blood
Sinew
Blubber
Antlers
Bird's Wing

The Inuit at Work and Play

The Inuit developed specific ways of making themselves comfortable and happy in their cold environment. The story on page 1 gives you an idea of the way they lived in extended families and how everyone in a community cared for one another. The men hunted, built their houses, made tools, and were able to cook. Women also knew how to hunt but spent most of their time cooking and sewing for the family. Children were educated by learning from adults around them.

The activities in this section focus on the Inuit's travels, houses, and play.

The A-mazing Inuit Cycle

From late spring until mid autumn, Qajaq and his family lived by themselves on land. Their summer home was on Baffin Island. There they lived in a tent and enjoyed the relative warmth of summer. They fished, hunted animals, and gathered berries and other plant foods. They also prepared for the coming winter.

In October or November, they traveled across the strait to live on the sea ice near the present town of Igloolik. (You can find Baffin Island and Igloolik on the map on the inside front cover.) There they lived in a community with other Inuit. They hunted together and shared their food. When the next spring arrived, they set off again for Baffin Island.

Their trips were often dangerous. Follow this maze as you travel with Qajaq's family from Baffin Island to Igloolik and back.

The Snowhouse Challenge

Here's how Qajaq's father and grandfather built their snowhouse (*igluvigaq,* eeg-LOO-vee-gack):

- First they marked a circle on the snow.
- Then they cut blocks of snow and positioned the first layer of blocks around the circle.
- They sliced six of these blocks to form a ramp. (This was the secret to making the snowhouse spiral into a dome.)
- Then they added the rest of the blocks. The last block at the very top was the key block.
- They filled in any spaces between the blocks with snow.
- Next they cut a small opening near the top for air to escape and a larger square hole for a block of ice that served as a window.
- Finally they cut a hole for an entrance and added a "porch."

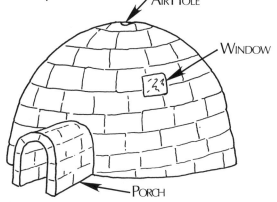

You can make a model of a snowhouse from homemade modeling dough. Here's how.

Materials

small mixing bowl or other dome-shaped object
plastic wrap
white cardboard (larger than bowl's diameter)
modeling dough (See column 2.)
white or clear glue
silver or white sparkles (optional)

Directions

1. Completely cover the outside of the mixing bowl (or other object) with plastic wrap.

2. Center the bowl on the cardboard.

3. Build your snowhouse over the bowl, following the steps that Qajaq's father and grandfather took in column 1. Note the following:

- Make small rectangles from the modeling dough for the snow blocks. Instead of slicing off the first six blocks, shape them as you model them. Pinch the blocks together as you work.
- Make a small air hole near the top.
- Build the "porch" (see illustration in column 1).
- If the dough shrinks, add more to close the gaps before the model dries.

4. After the model is dry, carefully remove a block for a window.

5. Drizzle glue over the snowhouse to make it sturdy. Add sparkles while the glue is wet.

6. When the glue is dry, remove the bowl.

7. Finally, glue a small piece of plastic wrap over the window to represent the block of ice.

8. You can model animals and people to complete your village.

Modeling Dough Recipe

1 1/2 cups (350 ml) flour
3 teaspoons (15 ml) cream of tartar
3/4 cup (180 ml) salt
3 tablespoons (45 ml) salad oil
1 1/2 cups (350 ml) water
adult to help

Mix dry ingredients in medium-size pot. Add oil and water. Cook mixture for 3-5 minutes over medium heat, stirring constantly until it forms a ball. When dough is cool enough to touch, knead it for a short time until it is firm and smooth. Add food coloring to mold people and animals. Store dough in a covered container.

Qajaq at Play

Qajaq and Ukpijuak spent much of their time learning from adults how to live in their cold environment. But they still had time to play-- often in their snowhouse during the long, dark winters. Here are some ways that you can have the kind of fun Qajaq and Ukpijuak had.

A Pushover

To play *arsuruniq* (ar-SOO-ruh-nirk), the game Qajaq and his friends played at the reunion in the *qaggiq* (KAH-gerk), you must first make the toy they used in the game.

Materials

antlers: Use 2 strong sticks about 4 inches
   (10 cm) long (for example, part of a broom
   handle or heavy dowel).
sinew: Use strong cord about 5 inches
   (12.5 cm) long.

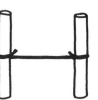

Tie the sticks together securely, as shown in this drawing.

Here's how to play. Find a partner about your size. Sit on the floor facing each other, so your feet touch your partner's and your legs are together and straight. You each hold one of the sticks with your right hand, being sure two fingers are above the string and two below. Keep your right arm as straight as possible. (See the picture on page 14.) On the count of three, you both pull backwards without bending either your arms or legs. The first one to be pulled over or to drop the toy loses that round.

Try an Inuit Poem

Turn to page 16 and read the poem that Uncle Qatalik sang at the reunion. Write a similar poem about a hunt, an animal, or an arctic trip.

Catch It if You Can

Inuit children played *ajajaq* (ai-YAH-yah). This toy consisted of a long, pointed object, often made of ivory, tied with sinew to a hollow bone or small mammal's skull. (See the outside back cover.) The object was to catch the bone or skull with the pointed stick. You can make an *ajajaq* too.

Materials

8-ounce (1/4-liter) paper cup
hole punch and scissors
dental floss
needle with large eye
transparent tape
pencil

1. Punch a hole in the cup between the rim and the base. Starting at the hole, cut an oval about 2 inches (5 cm) high and 3/4 inch (1.9 cm) wide. (See the illustration above.)

2. On the opposite side of the cup, cut a rectangle about 2 inches (5 cm) high but only 1/2 inch (1.3 cm) wide.

3. Thread the needle with a 20-inch (50 cm) length of dental floss and make a large knot at the longer end of the floss.

4. With the needle make a small hole in the center of the cup's bottom. Thread the dental floss through the hole from the *inside* of the cup and pull until the knot is tight against the cup.

5. Tape the knot to the inside of the cup.

6. Tie the pencil to the other end of the dental floss. (See the illustration.)

To play, hold the stick in one hand, letting the cup dangle. With an upward thrust, throw the cup into the air and try to catch it on the stick. Although the Inuit did not keep score, you can give yourself 5 points if you catch the oval hole, 10 points for the rectangular hole, and 15 points if the stick doesn't come out either hole.

Travel Tips

In some areas of northern Canada, the Inuit built a large type of boat called an *umiak* (OO-me-ack). They covered driftwood with walrus or seal skins to make boats that were 20 to 30 feet (6 to 9 m) long. These boats sometimes had removable sails, made from seal intestines sewn together.

When the Inuit traveled by water, the women, old men, and children rode in an *umiak*. The women either paddled or rowed the boat. Younger men paddled along in their kayaks.

The Igloolik Inuit rarely used this type of boat. Can you guess why? (See page 60 for the answer.)

Connect the dots to find out what an *umiak* looks like. (There are two pathways, ● and △ .) Then color the picture.

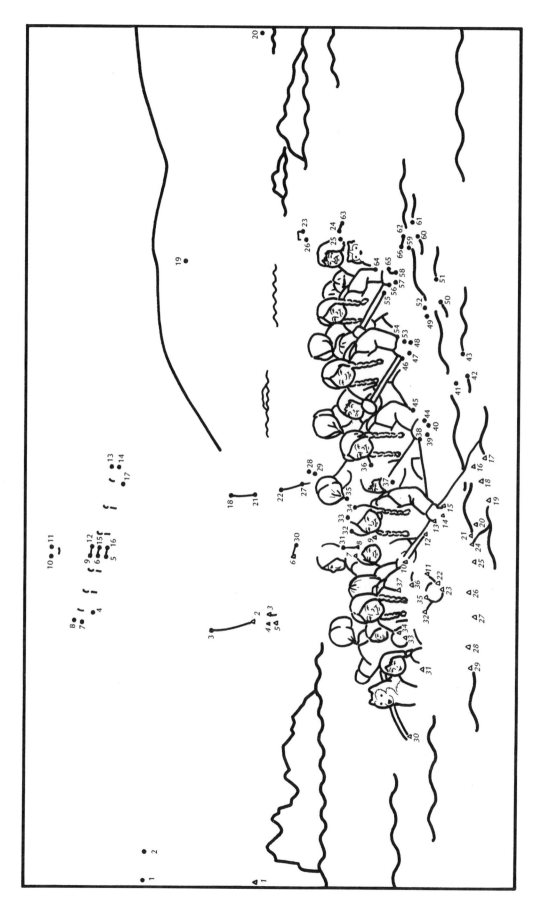

Calling All Arctic Experts!

How much did you learn as you read the story and had fun with the activities? You will use your knowledge of the Canadian Arctic in the next two activities. See how expert you are!

Did You Get the Drift?

Here are some words that you have learned as you read the story and did the activities throughout this book. Unfortunately, they are buried in a huge snowdrift! See how many you can dig out.

(You'll discover that some words are on the diagonal.) As you find the names, circle them. If you don't remember what they mean, look on page 59 or in a dictionary.

adaptation	cache	igluvigaq	parka	sinew	tundra
amautiq	caribou	Inuit	prey	sledge	ulu
amulet	carnivore	kakivak	qaggiq	snow goggles	umiak
blubber	harpoon	kayak	seal	tent	weir

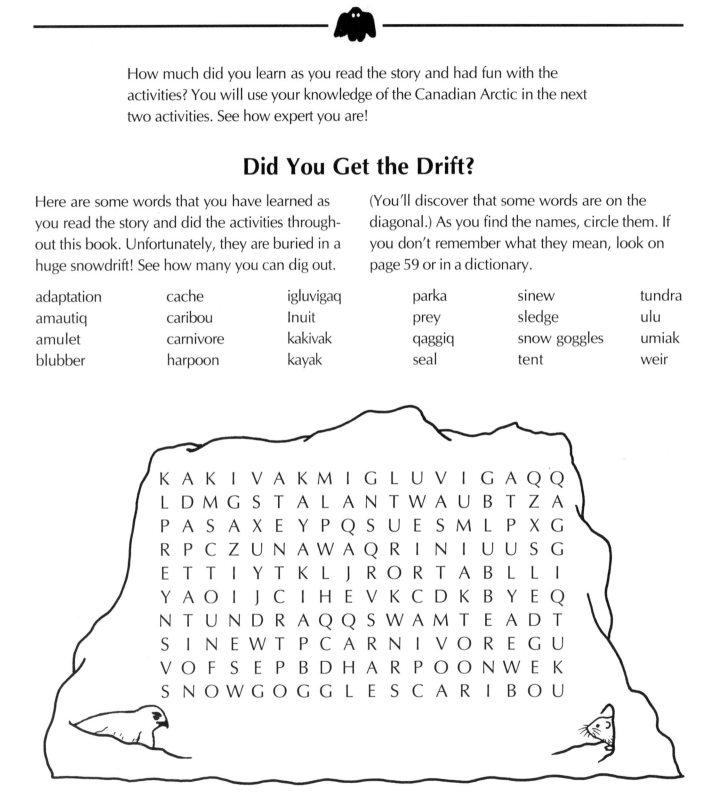

```
K A K I V A K M I G L U V I G A Q Q
L D M G S T A L A N T W A U B T Z A
P A S A X E Y P Q S U E S M L P X G
R P C Z U N A W A Q R I N I U U S G
E T T I Y T K L J R O R T A B L L I
Y A O I J C I H E V K C D K B Y E Q
N T U N D R A Q Q S W A M T E A D T
S I N E W T P C A R N I V O R E G U
V O F S E P B D H A R P O O N W E K
S N O W G O G G L E S C A R I B O U
```

Puppets for Playwrights

Now that you've read about the Arctic and the people who lived there around 1900, you can write your own arctic play. Here's what to do.

On the back cover of this book, you will find Qajaq and Ukpijuak in their summer seal skin clothing. You can turn them into puppets by cutting them out and taping a stick or spoon to the back of each. The ball, puppy, and *ajajaq* can be used as props, so cut them out too.

Next, color and cut out the children's winter caribou clothing on page 53. After you cut out the dog and sledge, make stands for them, using the instructions on page 53. You can also use the stands to move these props around.

If you've taken the challenge on page 47, you can use your snowhouse as a prop. Think of other props and characters you can make for your play. Finally, decide what to use as a stage. You could use a table, as shown on page 53.

Now you are ready to let your imagination take over. How many acts will you have? What will your plot be? Can you make up a tune for the poem you wrote on page 48? Who will your audience be?

What did the mother carnivore say when her daughter asked if she could have a friend for dinner? "Wouldn't it be better to have your enemy?"

Do *you* recognize him? He's not from *my* village.

Use a separate sheet of paper to draw your own arctic cartoons. Try them out on your friends.

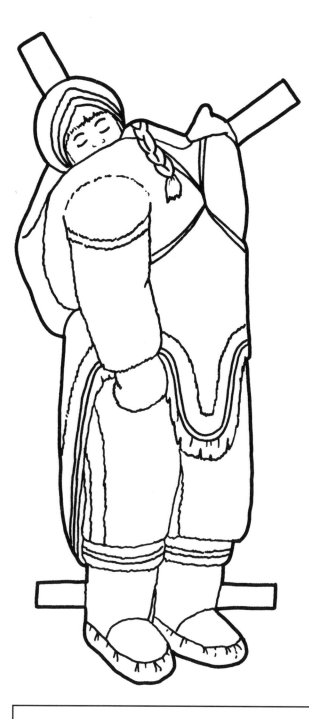

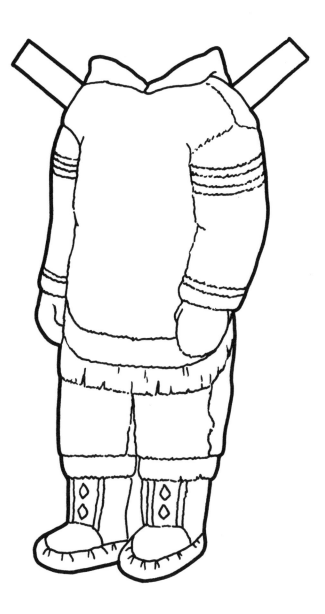

Prop Stands and Puppet Stage

Cut a strip of heavy construction paper or lightweight cardboard to the following dimensions: 1/2 inch x 10 inches (1.25 cm x 25 cm). Tape the ends together to make a circle. Tape the circle to the back of the dog in two places. (See the illustration.) Repeat these directions for the sledge. You can hold the stands to move these props across the stage.

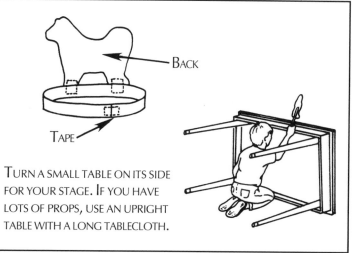

BACK

TAPE

TURN A SMALL TABLE ON ITS SIDE FOR YOUR STAGE. IF YOU HAVE LOTS OF PROPS, USE AN UPRIGHT TABLE WITH A LONG TABLECLOTH.

Setting the Scene for "The Arctic Today"

If you were to visit Igloolik today, you would find a permanent town of about 1,100 people near the place where Qajaq spent his winters on the sea ice. You would find local stores, churches, a community center, and a nursing station. The town has a mayor, and the Royal Canadian Mounted Police enforce the laws.

There is a school for children in kindergarten through grade 12. Young people like to ice skate at the rink and play volleyball. They also enjoy listening to the local radio station.

You would discover that the houses are usually made of wood with one, two, or three bedrooms. They are heated with oil and have electricity--but no sewers! Because of the permafrost (see page 22), they can't lay pipe lines underground. So they have to truck the waste away. They must also truck in water.

Join some of Qajaq's descendants as you read "Mikki's Promise" on page 55.

The Arctic Today: Mikki's Promise

Perched on a chair next to the window, tapping her feet on the floor, Mikki waited one more quiet minute before the guests arrived. She looked up at the balloons that she and Qajaq, laughing and popping a few, had hung from the ceiling earlier that day. She would miss her brother when he went to the university far south, but today would be fun. Relatives and friends would soon arrive for Qajaq's farewell party. Even his high school teachers were coming to celebrate, because not many students from Igloolik went to college. It seemed all of Igloolik was proud of Mikki's brother.

"Here they come!" Mikki called out as the first of the pickup trucks emerged from the cold August fog and pulled up next to their small frame house. A caravan of ATVs, and a few trucks followed behind.

One by one, each guest was greeted by Mother, Father, and Qajaq. Two by two, the sealskin boots and running shoes were lined up near the door. Mikki took her share of hugs from aunts and good-natured teasing from uncles.

"Ah, Mikki! How old are you now? Twenty-one?" Uncle George teased, although everybody knew she was ten!

Akishu (Ah-KEY-shoe), Mikki's thirteen-year-old sister, flipped through her cassettes and popped some rock music into the stereo. Mikki grabbed a handful of potato chips. As she ate, she hummed to herself and listened to the laughter and chatter of her family.

Uncle George cut a piece of caribou. "This," he told Mikki, "is from Baffin Island where I was hunting." To her father, he asked, "Was there news about Nunavut (New-NAH-voot) while I was gone?"

Nunavut means "our land." Mikki knew Nunavut was very important. It was the name of a territory being developed in Canada's north--a territory the Inuit themselves would govern. Father and Uncle George often talked about Inuit law, self-government, hunting rights, and mineral royalties. They debated how these issues would be dealt with in Nunavut. Although Mikki didn't understand such things very well, she knew that they were crucial to the future of her people.

Where's Grandmother? she wondered and then went looking. She found Grandmother sewing sealskin boots by hand in the bedroom.

"Grandmother! Why are you here all alone? Everyone's here! Qajaq's teachers are telling about the fine university he's going to!"

Grandmother shook her head. "Too many young ones go away," she said sadly. "Not to universities, maybe, but they still leave Igloolik. Now my Qajaq is going too. How can I be happy?"

"He'll be back to visit. Lots of times!" Mikki said.

"He could stay right here, be an outfitter like your father and take visiting hunters on dog team trips."

"He wants to be a lawyer, Grandmother. He has to go to school in the south."

Grandmother didn't listen. "Companies are always hiring men for oil exploration and mining. He doesn't have to go thousands of miles away."

"Qajaq says that kind of work is destroying the environment, Grandmother. Father also worries about the animals. The ships that carry oil frighten the sea animals. And you know the pipelines are above ground. They might block the caribou from following their migration routes." Mikki had often heard her father and Qajaq discuss these problems.

"Humph!" Grandmother responded. "Our people took care of the land very well for generations."

Mikki thought about this, about what it was like when Grandmother's father Qajaq, for whom her brother was named, was just her age. He ate food simmered in a soapstone pot. He lived in snowhouses and in tents, often far apart from other Inuit families for long seasons. Mikki sat on the floor, hugging her knees.

"I like being near my friends all year long. I like watching TV and playing Nintendo with them. And I like going to the gym and the ice skating rink," Mikki stressed. "Summer camp was fun on Baffin Island, where you grew up, Grandmother. But I like Igloolik. And I like school."

Grandmother raised her eyebrows.

"Most of the time," Mikki added.

"TV, Nintendo," Grandmother muttered. "And what is happening to our language? Young people don't speak *Inuktitut* very well anymore."

"We learn *Inuktitut* in school," exclaimed Mikki. "And you know that you and the other elders come to class to show us things you learned when you were young--like kayak-making and cooking. All the kids love to hear you tell the stories that have been passed down from long ago, when our people had no written language."

Grandmother pushed her needle through the skin. She was quiet for a few moments, then said softly, "I suppose you'll leave, too, when you are older."

Mikki hadn't thought about that! How could she ever leave Igloolik, her home, her friends, her family?

"Oh no, Grandmother," Mikki said, looking earnestly into the old woman's sad eyes. "I won't ever leave, I promise." The thought of leaving scared her, and she wondered for a moment whether Qajaq, who always seemed so brave, was frightened about going away.

"Grandmother! There you are!" It was Qajaq, leaning in the doorway. "Come," he said gently. "My teachers would like to meet you."

Grandmother laid her work aside and stood. She placed her hands on his strong shoulders and studied his face as though memorizing it. "My Little Father, going away," she said. Her eyes brimmed with tears.

"I'll be back before you know it!" Qajaq said, brushing a tear from her cheek. "It's easy to travel now. I'll come on the plane! You won't be rid of your Little Father so easily."

Grandmother looked at him doubtfully.

"There will be work concerning Nunavut for a long, long time," Qajaq added. "Important decisions will be made about our land, not only about its surface but about underground resources as well. When I finish school, I'm going to be a part of all that--to help preserve our land."

"But you won't be here," Grandmother protested.

"Probably not, but I will visit often," Qajaq assured her. "I won't be too far away. Think how important my work will be to all of us."

Grandmother sighed deeply. She hadn't thought of his leaving in that way. Finally, she said in a quiet voice, "Our people and the land have always been one. I am glad you will continue to be part of it. If you must go, I will try to understand."

Mikki had not thought of Qajaq's leaving in that way either. She knew that the Inuit way of life had always come from the land and from the animals that lived on it. Her brother wanted to learn how to preserve the land and protect the animals. How proud of him she was!

"What can I do for the land?" Mikki asked, also wanting to help.

"One day you will know, Little Sister," Qajaq assured her. "But there is something very important you can do right now."

"What is it?" she asked, watching her brother's face light up.

"Help me take Grandmother to the party."

Grandmother protested only a moment as Qajaq and Mikki each took an arm. Then together they went to join the guests.

Words to Remember

adaptation. The ability to change that helps plants, animals, and humans to survive in their environments.

amautiq (ah-MAO-tee). A parka worn by women and older girls. It has a pouch in the back for carrying a baby.

amulet. A charm to help or protect the wearer.

Arctic. The area north of the Arctic Circle.

cache. A storage place for food or goods. Many animals hide food in caches. The Inuit stored some possessions in caches for safe-keeping before their seasonal moves.

igluvigaq (eeg-LOO-vee-gack). A house made of blocks of snow. The plural is *igluvigat*.

Inuit. The name for people of Canada and Alaska who were formerly called *Eskimo*.

Inuktitut (ee-NOOK-tee-toot). The oral and written language of the Inuit.

kakivak (KA-kee-vack). A fishing spear with prongs. (See the second page of this book.)

qaggiq (KAH-gerk). A large structure used for social gatherings.

soapstone lamp. A shallow stone bowl for burning oil to warm a house, cook food, and dry clothes.

sinew. A tendon of an animal. The Inuit used sinew like thread for sewing.

strait. A narrow body of water connecting two large bodies of water.

tundra. The treeless desert of the arctic region.

weir. A dam made of rocks built to trap fish. The Inuit would then spear them with a *kakivak*.

Other Books to Read

Andrews, Jan. *Very Last First Time.* New York: Atheneum, 1986.

Fictional story of an Inuit girl as she searches for mussels in the seabed under the ice.

Bramwell, Martyn. *Glaciers and Ice Sheets.* New York: Franklin Watts, 1986.

Includes a chapter on the Arctic and a glossary.

Ferris, Jeri. *Arctic Explorer: The Story of Matthew Henson.* Minneapolis: Carolrhoda Books, 1989.

The biography of Henson, the black man on Robert Peary's expedition that reached the North Pole. For age 11 and up.

Field, Edward. *Eskimo Songs and Stories.* New York: Delacorte Press/S. Lawrence, 1973.

Selection of material collected by Knud Rasmussen on an arctic expedition.

Houston, James. *Frozen Fire.* New York: Atheneum, 1977.

Adventure story for readers age 11 and up.

_____ . *Songs of the Dream People.* New York: Atheneum, 1972.

Songs of the Inuit and other Native American groups.

Hunt, Patricia. *Snowy Owls.* New York: Dodd, Mead & Co., 1982.

The natural history of snowy owls, illustrated with photographs.

Maher, Ramona. *The Blind Boy and the Loon and Other Eskimo Myths.* New York: The John Day Company, 1969.

Myths of the Alaskan and Canadian Inuit, with ilustrations of original Inuit artworks.

Patent, Dorothy Hinshaw. *Seals, Sea Lions and Walruses.* New York: Holiday House, 1990.

Contains substantial interesting information about aquatic animals called pinnipeds, including a chapter on the future of seals.

Steiner, Barbara. *Whale Brother.* New York: Walker and Company, 1988.

A young boy wants to create great carvings, but he does not understand how to put "life" into them until he stands watch by a dying whale. Fiction.

Yue, Charlotte and David. *The Igloo.* Boston: Houghton Mifflin, 1988.

Describes the arctic environment, snowhouse construction, and Inuit traditional life. Good illustrations and bibliography.

Answers

Page 22
The lid that faces the lamp directly receives the rays of light head-on, so it receives the most light and heat. It represents the Equator. Because the angled lid does not face the lamp directly, it receives less light and heat than the other lid. It represents the Arctic.

Page 24   Igloolik Answers:

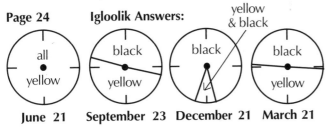

all yellow — June 21
black / yellow — September 23
black / yellow & black — December 21
black / yellow — March 21

Pages 26-32
Collared lemming: When there are fewer lemmings, there are fewer animals that eat the lemming. When lemmings are plentiful, the other animals are plentiful.

Ermine: thick fur; short ears and legs; stores food; builds den; changes color.

Arctic ground squirrel: thick fur; short ears, tail, and legs; eats lots of food; stores food; winters under snow; hibernates.

Arctic hare: thick fur; furry feet; short ears and tail; sharp claws; sometimes changes color.

Arctic fox: long, thick fur; short ears and legs; eats lots of food; sharp claws; changes color.

Gray wolf: thick fur; furry feet; short ears; stores food; builds den; sharp claws.

Caribou: long, thick fur; furry feet; short ears and tail; migrates. Wide feet help this animal run on snow.

Musk-ox: long, thick fur; furry feet; short ears, tail, and legs; eats lots of food.

Polar bear: thick fur; furry feet; short ears, tail, and legs; eats lots of food; builds den; sharp claws.

Ringed seal: oily, waterproof skin; thin fur; blubber; sharp claws.

Narwhal: oily, waterproof skin; blubber; migrates.

Walrus: thin fur; blubber; migrates.

Beluga whale: oily, waterproof skin; blubber, migrates.

Bowhead whale: oily, waterproof skin; blubber; migrates.

Willow ptarmigan: lots of feathers; feathers on feet and ankles; burrows in snow; changes color; eats lots of food.

Snowy owl: lots of feathers; feathers on feet and ankles; sometimes migrates; eats lots of food.

Snow goose: lots of feathers; migrates; eats lots of food.

Page 33
arctic fox, ermine, willow ptarmigan, and lemmings. (The arctic hare sometimes does, depending on its location.)

Page 36

Food Chain A
olfw = wolf
ctiacr xfo = arctic fox
oubicar = caribou
mligenm = lemming
tacric reha = arctic hare
skmu-xo = musk-ox
riccat rogudn lisqurer = arctic ground squirrel
ctiacr raeh = arctic hare
immleng = lemming
gaptrmian = ptarmigan
sncetsi = insects
paltns = plants   talpns = plants

Food Chain B
oppele = people
begaul ewahl = beluga whale
asle = seal
qudsi = squid
hisf = fish
ellisfhsh = shellfish
poolnkzaont = zooplankton
ppoonntthyalk = phytoplankton

Page 42
Because in the Arctic there is little sunlight in winter.

Page 44

Skin	**Ivory**	**Blood**	**Antlers**
boat cov-erings	harpoons	bait	*ajajaq*
parkas	amulets		snow beaters
tents	needles	**Sinew**	seal probes
blankets	snow goggles	bow strings	knives
amulets	combs	*ajajaq* thread	
			Bird's Wing
Bone	**Meat**	**Blubber**	amulets
knives	bait	food	
ajajaq	food	oil	
	dog food		

Page 46

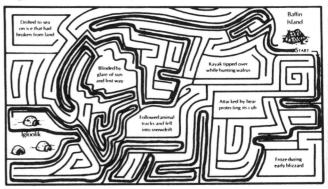

Page 49
No trees grow in Igloolik, so wood was scarce.

Page 50

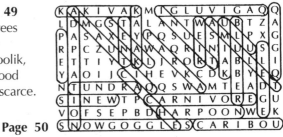